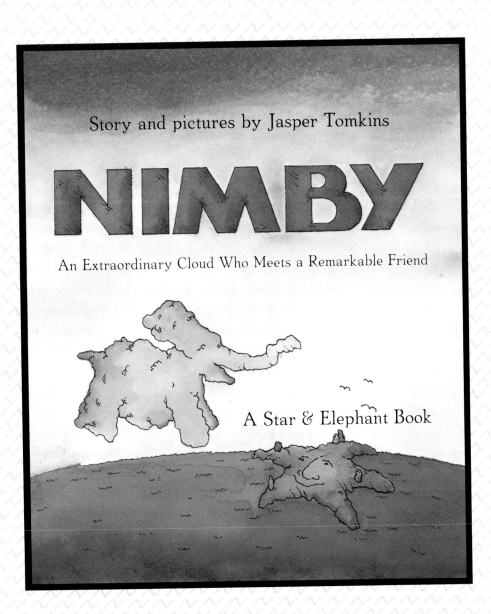

Story and pictures by Jasper Tomkins

NIMBY

An Extraordinary Cloud Who Meets a Remarkable Friend

A Star & Elephant Book

Story and pictures copyright ©1982 by Jasper Tomkins
Green Tiger Press, Box 3000, La Jolla, California 92038
ISBN 0-914676-83-0
First Edition · Second Printing

To the full moon
rolling up the back
of Goblin Knob.

One gleaming day a magical wave crashed against the shore rocks of a faraway sea.

As the spray rose into the air it became a small cloud which flew higher and higher, just like a bird. This new cloud was welcomed to the sky by some grand old puffs. They named him Nimby.

Nimby was the darling of the cloud family, but they soon found that he was truly a special cloud.

When the old ones said, "Today we will all be tall and proud and fluffy," Nimby felt like sliding on the mountain tops.

When the sky was to be full of little white fluffs, Nimby was a long flowing spiral.

And when everyone spread out together to make a thick fog, Nimby was a great golden fish.

When the clouds were high and thin,
Nimby was a happy pig.

And when the sky was full of graceful popcorn clouds, Nimby was a comfy couch.

When the clouds swelled up dark and poured down rain, Nimby was a plane and made a hole to let the sun shine through.

This was too much! "Clouds are beautiful when they are shaped by the sky and wind," said the big old puffs.

"But playfulness is a step beyond beauty," replied Nimby.

"Harumph!" grumbled the old ones, even though some of them were secretly delighted.

The next day Nimby was a tree. He sat all day on a mountaintop until the cloud family finally moved on. "Goodbye," he said to no one in particular, and then he sailed off alone.

Soon Nimby came to a city. He made stars and even changed colors, but no one noticed. Everyone was too busy.

Nimby found some children in the countryside and stopped to make animals for them.

But the hills soon became grumpy because Nimby was blocking the afternoon sun. The children were frightened and ran away. Nimby threw some lightening down at the grumbling hills and then sailed away as the thunder rumbled.

Nimby was discouraged. He shut his eyes and let the wind blow him wherever it pleased.

When Nimby finally opened his eyes he was in the middle of the ocean. It was very lonely. He sighed and sailed on.

When he opened his eyes again he saw
a tiny speck far ahead on the ocean. As
he got closer he saw that it was a little
island, all alone.

But as he looked, the island turned into a ship. Nimby could hardly believe his eyes.

Then the ship became a baseball mitt. Nimby was overjoyed! He sailed down to be the ball.

Nimby and the island were a wonderful pair. Every day they would surprise each other with new tricks.

They made ice cream floats.

And mysterious castles.

And rainbows.

And fountains.

And smoke rings.

And even bananas.

But if they saw a ship or the cloud family nearby, they would quickly become just two little islands alone in the sea.

Nimby and the island were the best of friends. And no one ever knew, except you, and me, and the sun.

Color separations by Photolitho, AG of Zurich, Switzerland.
Text was set in Artcraft Light by Typecast of San Diego.
Printed at The Green Tiger Press, La Jolla, California.